4/03

A Note to Parents and Caregivers:

Read-it! Joke Books are for children who are moving ahead on the amazing road to reading. These fun books support the acquisition and extension of reading skills as well as a love of books.

Published by the same company that produces *Read-it!* Readers, these books introduce the question/answer pattern that helps children expand their thinking about language structure and book formats.

When sharing a book with your child, read in short stretches, pausing often to talk about the pictures and the meaning of the book. The question/answer format works well for this purpose and provides an opportunity to talk about the language and meaning of the jokes. Have your child turn the pages and point to the pictures and familiar words. Read the story in a natural voice; have fun creating the voices of characters or emphasizing some important words. And be sure to re-read favorite parts.

There is no right or wrong way to share books with children. Find time to read with your child and pass on the legacy of literacy.

Adria F. Klein, Ph.D.
Professor Emeritus
California State University
San Bernardino, California

Look for the other books in this series:

Animal Quack-Ups: Foolish and Funny Jokes About Animals (1-4048-0125-1)
Dino Rib Ticklers: Hugely Funny Jokes About Dinosaurs (1-4048-0122-7)
Galactic Giggles: Far-Out and Funny Jokes About Outer Space (1-4048-0126-X)
Monster Laughs: Frightfully Funny Jokes About Monsters (1-4048-0123-5)
School Buzz: Classy and Funny Jokes About School (1-4048-0121-9)

Editor: Nadia Higgins
Designer: John Moldstad
Page production: Picture Window Books
The illustrations in this book were prepared digitally.

Picture Window Books
5115 Excelsior Boulevard
Suite 232
Minneapolis, MN 55416
1-877-845-8392
www.picturewindowbooks.com

Printed in the United States of America.
1 2 3 4 5 6 08 07 06 05 04 03

Library of Congress Cataloging-in-Publication Data
Dahl, Michael.
Chewy chuckles : deliciously funny jokes about food /
written by Michael Dahl ; illustrated by Jeff Yesh.
p. cm. — (Read-it! Joke Books)
Summary: An easy-to-read collection of jokes about strawberries,
alphabet soup, and other foods.
ISBN 1-4048-0124-3 (library binding)
1. Food—Juvenile humor. 2. Wit and humor, Juvenile. [1. Food—Humor.
2. Riddles. 3. Jokes.] I. Yesh, Jeff, 1971- ill. II. Title. III. Series.
PN6231.F66 D34 2003
818'.5402—dc21
                                                        2002156404

Chewy
Chuckles

Deliciously Funny Jokes About Food

Michael Dahl • Illustrated by Jeff Yesh

Reading Advisers:
Adria F. Klein, Ph.D.
Professsor Emeritus, California State University
San Bernardino, California

Susan Kesselring, M.A., Literacy Educator
Rosemount-Apple Valley-Eagan (Minnesota) School District

PICTURE WINDOW BOOKS
Minneapolis, Minnesota

What did one tomato say to the other tomato?

"You run on ahead, and I'll ketchup." 5

What do ducks eat for lunch?

Soup and quackers.

Why did the cookie go to the doctor?

It felt a little crummy.

What do you call
a sad strawberry?

A blue berry.

Why did the banana go to the doctor?

It wasn't peeling well. 9

If you throw a pumpkin up in the air, what comes down?

Squash.

What has bread on both sides and is scared of the dark?

A chicken sandwich.

Why did the student eat his homework?

The teacher told him it
was a piece of cake.

Where do cookies sleep?

On cookie sheets.

Why did the lettuce and tomato blush?

They saw the salad dressing.

Why did the orange
lose the race?

It ran out of juice.   17

How do you make a banana shake?

Take it to a scary movie.

What do you call cheese that doesn't belong to you?

Nacho cheese.

Why was the raspberry crying?

All his friends were in a jam.

What do you call two banana peels?

A pair of slippers.

"Waitress! What's this fly
doing in my alphabet soup?"

"I think it's learning to read."

What's the best day to have a cookout?

Fry day!